Yes Sister

Alice Love

Sketches by Alice Love

Alice Love Publications

ISBN: 979-8-89175-120-0 (sc)
ISBN: 979-8-89175-121-7 (hc)
ISBN: 979-8-89175-122-4 (ebk)

Yes Sister

For Ken

Thanks

My special thanks to every Sister, who by example and personal tuition, helped to turn inexperienced young women into professional trained nurses.

A big thank you too, to all our family and friends for all their help, support and personal interactions over the years; adding colour and texture to the tapestry of our lives.

Forward

By 1947 the second-world-war was over. One of the few benefits, that came directly as a result of its ravages; was the advancement in restorative and cosmetic surgery, as broken bodies and disfigured faces were restored to a semblance of normality.

This was an important starting place for the restoration of tortured minds.

Sulphonamides and penicillin were saving many lives that would have previously been lost to infection.

One of our medical lecturers emphasized "When you finally realize how little you know, you are then in a position to acquire a little knowledge".

The advances in all branches of the Medical Profession since then have been phenomenal. No doubt in another seventy years, someone else will say the same thing!

At that time in New Zealand, most of the larger Public Hospitals were staffed mainly by trainee nurses. Many of those who came through this system of training, believe that there were many benefits gained from the interaction with our patients, at all stages of the course.

This is a record of our lives between 1947 and 1956 from my perspective.

Preliminary

"NURSE!"

Sister's stentorian voice echoed down the ward between two rows of beds lined up with military precision against the walls. Two rows of bored ex-servicemen glanced in the direction she was glaring, with varying amounts of interest and sympathy.

One highly embarrassed young country girl, with face the same bright pink as her very new uniform, stood at attention and responded "Yes Sister?" before rectifying the minor misdemeanor she had so obviously committed.

The war had been over for nearly two years, but it was going to take a lot longer than that to repair the bodies and minds of many young men.

Twenty or more of these were recuperating in one ward under the very able care of a Sister who had spent the war years overseas in military hospitals.

I was very lucky to have been sent to this ward as my first real nursing experience. Sister was very strict, but fair and a good teacher, with a real empathy with her patients.

On April 4th 1947 with twenty six other new girls I commenced my nursing training

We were accommodated in an old manse, and in my room were three other girls, Phil Wright, Eileen Keen and Barbara Watson.

We remained close friends throughout our training years; and with Eileen and Phil for many years after. Barbara didn't complete her training and we lost touch.

We were not permitted to use Christian names on the wards and were advised to get out of the habit of doing so. From then on it was usually Wright, Keen, Watson and Thomson.

On the wards the prefix was Nurse. In the lecture room we were seated alphabetically, and Lenore Taylor became the fifth in our group, and my best friend.

Lenore was an only child who lived in the city, and when our days off coincided, Mr. and Mrs. Taylor acquired a second daughter.

As we had already been measured for our uniforms on the day we were interviewed and had a medical exam, these uniforms were waiting for us. There was a pink cotton dress with long sleeves, a large white apron with straps that crossed at the back and buttoned at the side waist, and a stiffly starched white collar to be attached with a collar stud to the front neck of the dress—we quickly learned to soften the neck edge of that collar by rubbing a dry cake of soap along it. There were stiffly starched white cuffs held in cylindrical shape by a stud.

These cuffs were always worn, except for any task where it was necessary to roll up ones sleeves. A stiffly starched white belt held by the usual stud, and a specially shaped piece of white cotton material that folded into a cap with a starched turned up brim completed the uniform. The cap was also held together with a stud and affixed to our hair with two hair clips. Hair had to be short or firmly secured under one's cap.

As I had long hair [which I already wore in two long braids wrapped round my head], I didn't have to make any changes. Jewelry, makeup and nail polish were not to be even considered.

We had to supply our own black stockings and black, low heeled, lace up shoes.

There was also a navy blue woollen cape with long straps that crossed over one's chest and fastened under the cape at the back.

The first day was very busy and flew by, but in the evening homesickness set in. I went to the phone and rang home. Dad answered, and I very nearly burst into tears. After a few minutes chat I was fine again.

Our first three months were filled with lectures and practicing nursing techniques. On Saturday afternoons we would go in pairs to one of the wards for two hours, to observe and assist with suitable duties like giving out afternoon tea and feeding patients.

We were seconded to sing in the choir for Choral Matins in the chapel on Sunday mornings, and this involved some evening practices. Before the Sunday service we would go to the wards to collect any wheelchair patients who wished to attend the service, and then return them after the service.

By the time we started training, a cleaning company was employed to clean the wards.

The only cleaning we did was in the sterilizing room, and dealing with any spills or breakages as they occurred. However, part of our training was involved with ward cleaning, and a section of the training school where we had our lectures, was divided into small cubicles, each containing a brass door handle.

Each morning we would have to clean and polish our own cubicle to a standard that would pass Sister's inspection.

One morning I arrived at the school slightly early, and made a start on my cleaning. With extra time, I gave my piece of floor an extra polish; and stood back to admire the clean and shining floor and the gleaming brass before repairing to my desk to do some revision. The rest of the class arrived and did their cleaning, and then Sister arrived and made her inspection. She looked over the cubicles and called me over. "Nurse Thomson! Have you done your cleaning?"

"Yes Sister"

"Come and look at this!" She then proceeded to berate me for laziness and dishonesty. I hadn't considered the fact that when the rest of the class vigorously swept and polished their cubicles, a certain amount of dust would rise in the air, and some of it would settle undisturbed on the floor of my cubicle, awaiting Sister's inspection!

During the three months of preliminary instruction we did not have any overnight leave.

Close to the end of this time there was the annual Nurses' Ball, held at the Winter Garden venue. I didn't have anyone I wished to invite, so one of the girls arranged a blind date for me. We were both shy people but had quite a pleasant evening. We didn't arrange a second meeting.

All of our class passed the exam at the end of the course and we were now junior probationary nurses.

Our pink uniform was exchanged for a grey one, and we were each appointed to a ward. There were three different shifts—morning from six am until two pm—afternoon from two pm until ten pm—and a divided shift that covered the busiest times of both morning and afternoon.

These shifts were rotated, and it was always necessary to look at the duty roster on the nurses' home notice board, to see which shift one was on, or if it was our day off. We also moved from the Manse to the nurses' old home.

Prior to leaving Manahune, Aunt Dorothy had arranged a farewell afternoon for me at her place. All the local ladies were there and they presented me with a very nice leather weekend bag. This bag now came into use for my occasional visits home.

Sometimes Dad would pick me up and bring me back to the hospital.

At least twice when I found I had two nights off, I caught the road services bus on Victoria St and would be let off at the Waipara hotel. I then walked the six and a half miles up to Manahune [the farm where I was raised] and would come in through the front door and leave my bag in the bedroom. I would then make my entry into the kitchen through the hall door, and surprise whoever happened to be in the kitchen.

Later when I had my bicycle at the nurses' home, I set out to bike as far as I could until Dad met me. Going via Forfar St, McSaveney's Rd and Marshland's Rd, I got as far as Kaiapoi.

Lectures continued, and one could attend either the morning or afternoon lecture to fit in with one's shift. A day off did not excuse one from lectures. In general I enjoyed lectures and tests.

During one lecture a male Doctor expressed his opinion that women's period pains were purely psychological. The unspoken wish list from his audience was anatomically impossible!

It was necessary to do a fair amount of swotting, and when the weather was nice, there were plenty of delightful spots in the hospital grounds, or the botanic gardens where we could repair with our books.

On one lovely day I was sitting against a tree beside the river in the gardens. I was quite engrossed with what I was reading, but I suddenly noticed I was not alone. Five delightful baby weasels had come out to play. I kept very still and they chased each other all around my legs, tumbling over each other and playing just like kittens, before disappearing as suddenly as they had arrived.

<h1 style="text-align:center">Year One</h1>

After my preliminary training I spent three months in the returned services ward, and then six months in men's surgical.

For my first annual leave I spent the fortnight at Manahune.

My three months junior night duty was in the women's orthopaedic ward. There were quite a few elderly ladies who had fractured the necks of their femurs.

To enable them to pull themselves up in their beds, ropes had been attached to the ceiling above each bed. A wooden handle with a hole through the middle was threaded onto the rope, and held in place with a single overhand knot.

While my senior nurse was away from the ward to have her dinner, I did a round of the ward and found one of my patients sitting up in bed, very busily unknotting the rope holding her handle.

" What are you doing? Dear."

"I'm going to get that night nurse!"

I didn't think it necessary to tell her that I was the night nurse, as I confiscated the ten inch piece of wood and stored it on the desk for the rest of the night.

When she awoke in the morning she was her usual sweet tempered self.

She was no doubt surprised to see me reattaching her handle before I went off duty.

Before going off duty at six in the morning, the night staff would have given bed pans to all patients confined to their beds.

In an orthopaedic ward this could mean the majority of the patients. Most would also have to be assisted on and off the pans, and, depending on the disability, two nurses could be required. It was necessary to commence this task no later than a quarter past five in the morning.

The sterilizing room was on one side in the middle of the ward. One morning I warmed, covered, and picked up a pile of five stainless steel bedpans and walked out into the centre of the ward. For some reason I lost my balance and five metal bedpans landed on the floor.

It was not necessary to wake anyone up that morning!

As I went off duty I had to deliver a message to the ward immediately underneath—a men's medical ward. The men were all awake and very irate because of the terrible racket from upstairs.

The patients' meals were cooked in the hospital kitchen about half way along the main corridor and the cooked individual items were sent to the ward in large stainless steel, lidded containers that fitted into a heated trolley. Cold foods sat in a cupboard at the base of the trolley.

The patients' lockers would have been opened out and set with cutlery in plenty of time; and as soon as the trolley arrived in the ward, Sister and staff nurse would start dishing out the meals. The rest of the staff would deliver them to the patients as quickly as possible, so they wouldn't get cold.

Before we started serving the meal we would have rolled down our sleeves and put on our cuffs. When everybody had a meal we would feed anyone who needed help.

Some special diets came from the diet kitchen already dished. The food was ample and flavoursome, and Sister made sure it was attractively served. Most patients were very happy with their meals. Usually the ones who complained would have preferred their usual diet of fish and chips and pies.

After the meal we took the dirty dishes to the ward kitchen on a trolley and the ward maid did the washing up, by hand.

In some of the older ward kitchens, there was a small, round, steam heated water bath in which containers could be heated.

An early afternoon task was to fill a one gallon enamel jug with cubes of bread, and top it up with milk.

This sat in the water bath for the afternoon, and the patients had the option of some hot bread and milk for their tea. There were never any leftovers.

Whenever there were leftover items from breakfast, after the patients had been served; these would be put in the refrigerator, and when it was time for me to make morning tea for Sister, and any Doctors making ward rounds, there would be a variety of options. Prune and bacon sandwiches were always a hit!

Each trainee nurse spent a few days working in the hospital kitchen and diet kitchen, during their training. I was amazed when I first saw a large, washing machine sized, bowl of potatoes being mashed with an electric beater. My most enduring memories of those kitchens are from night duty days. My route back to the nurses' home, just after six in the morning, led past the hospital kitchens.

I would make a detour and make myself two large squares of hot buttered toast with a generous spread of marmalade. By the time I reached my room I had finished my breakfast.

The nurses' meals were cooked and eaten in the nurses' new home. There was a large dining room with tables that seated six. On the opposite side to the kitchen, in the centre of that side of the room, was a smaller table where Matron would sit, usually accompanied by her two most senior staff members.

We would stand when Matron entered the room, and again when she rose to leave. If one was late for a meal one would pause and stand at attention in the aisle opposite this main table, until Matron or whoever was her deputy, acknowledged one's presence with a nod.

One only shared a table with staff of one's own rank, and a waitress had been heard to remark that she never had to look at the uniforms to know which group she was serving. At one table the discussion was about bedpans; at another it would be injections and dressings. If the topic was rather lurid anatomical details, it was safe to assume that those girls were doing a stint in the operating theatre.

The food was good, plentiful and tasty. There was a tendency for certain menus to repeat on the same day of the week. It was a standing joke that we always had kidneys on Tuesdays. Everyone knew that urinary tract operations were only performed on a Monday.

Two things, for which I developed a permanent liking, then, were cooked tomatoes and kidneys.

An important duty for the most junior nurses, was putting pillows and woollen blankets outside in the sun on fine days. These would have to be turned over during the day, and of course brought inside again before there was any hint of moisture in the air.

Beds, rubber sheeting and lockers were wiped over with antiseptic after any patient had returned home.

Bed making was a finely honed art much practiced in preliminary school. A chair would be placed at the foot of the bed to receive the bedclothes. Nothing was allowed to touch the floor. The sides and ends of the bed were untucked, the pillows were placed on the chair, then each item of bedding was individually folded back to the foot of the bed, then with a hand each end of the midline of the item it was lifted off the bed, so it was folded in four, and placed neatly over the back of the chair.

This stripping of a bed could be accomplished very fast, especially with a nurse each side, and the woollen blankets pulled quickly over the metal bed frame created some amazing static electricity—a trap for the first person touching the bed frame thereafter.

The bed was remade just as efficiently, and the white bedspread was finished with precision mitred hospital corners.

For the privacy of the patients the beds could be surrounded by threefold-screens. These were a wooden frame covered with a removable white cotton cover.

A fair amount of time and energy was expended carrying these screens around the ward and putting them away after use.

Essentials

AN ESSENTIAL IN EVERY WARD was the thermometer tray. A thermometer for each patient in the ward, sat in a test tube containing antiseptic solution, in a row on each side of the tray.

At either end between the rows were containers for clean and used cotton wool swabs. Because it took at least a minute for the thermometer to record an accurate reading, it was customary to give out three or four thermometers at a time.

The antiseptic was wiped off with a clean swab, and the thermometer read and shaken down to a lower than normal temperature, before being inserted under the patient's tongue. The shake down was accomplished with a flick of the wrist, and care was needed to avoid contact with hard surfaces in the vicinity.

The slim glass tubes were quite fragile, and bumps, drops or bites ended the lives of some of them. Over-heating could also cause a breakage.

During the wait time one would take the pulse and respiration rates, then record them on the patient's chart.

The thermometer was finally removed from the patient's mouth and read, before wiping it and returning it to its test tube. The temperature was charted, and this procedure was repeated until everyone had been attended to.

Occasionally, when one retrieved the thermometer from an otherwise fit looking [and sounding] patient, one would read a temperature that indicated his imminent demise. After checking his locker for the presence of a hot drink, one would retake his temperature, under strict supervision all the time. This time, it was invariably, perfectly normal.

Essentials for the nurses were an easily read pocket watch, with a sweep second hand, for timing pulse and respiration rates. This had a short chain that was pinned beside the pocket. There was also a pair of blunt ended scissors that had a multitude of uses.

They were private property and were usually engraved with, at least, initials. Pinned to the top edge of our big pocket was a chain of assorted safety pins. The length of the chain was determined by which ward one was working in.

Very important was a fountain pen in one's top pocket; necessary for charting. During the latter part of our training there was a directive to the effect that, if anybody owned one of those 'new-fangled' ball point pens, it was on no account to be used for charting. This important task was to be done only with proper pen and ink.

Apparently there was a fear over the permanence of the new ink. It would be 'a scandal' if a chart was opened X number of years later, and it was completely blank!

Other essentials were an empathy with our patients and a dedication to our calling. A good sense of humour was a very definite asset.

Year Two

BANDAGES WERE WASHED AT THE hospital and had to be rolled ready for use–a rather time consuming task–more easily accomplished with two people. Sometimes a bored long term patient would be very happy to take over this task. Dressings were made by the nurses, and cotton wool balls were rolled into swabs, ready for a multitude of uses. Dressings, dressing sheets and swabs were put into autoclave drums and sent to the operating theatre to be sterilized in the autoclave.

The autoclave could be put to other uses. In one ward near the theatres, the afternoon staff would occasionally supply the theatre staff with an egg, some sugar and some cream; and receive in return a share of the very delectable meringues, for supper.

Part way through the early part of our training we graduated to senior probationary nurses, and wore a white triangle on the sleeve to acknowledge this.

Half way through the course we sat the junior state exam, and as junior nurses, the triangle was replaced with a white stripe.

On Sundays, if I was not on morning duty, I would go to Church. If I was short of time I would attend the service in the Nurses' Chapel, wearing uniform; or change into mufti and cross the street to Saint Andrew's Presbyterian Church. This was situated in the triangle bounded by Tuam Street, Antigua Street and Oxford Terrace.

When time was not an issue, I would walk down Riccarton Avenue to Saint James's Anglican Church where Mum's cousins, the Hamilton family, were regular attendants. Twice I walked into Cathedral Square in time for Matins in the Cathedral.

The music was lovely, but if one attempted to join in singing a hymn, the glares from neighbouring pews indicated that it was not the 'done' thing.

When Lenore and I were at her home, we would accompany her Mum to the Opawa Methodist Church.

About ten girls from our class belonged to the Nurses' Christian Union, and met one evening a week in someone's room. Usually about five would attend, as the rest would be on duty. There was only one chair, so most would sit on the bed, or on cushions on the floor. With this group I went to an evening service at the Church of Christ; and another time we joined a group of University Christians for a combined meeting at the university students' union building.

I didn't have my bicycle at the hospital until I moved to the nurses' new home after about fifteen months.

There was a large basement underneath where bikes could be stored.

The tramcar only cost one penny from the hospital to the Square. This was a special rate–that only applied to this part of the route. I usually walked, mainly to save my pennies! On occasions I have been known to go for a walk on my own in the city, turning alternately left and right, to see where I finished up.

Mum's best friend, Auntie Margaret, and her husband, Uncle Harold Southerill lived at 13 Hoonhay Rd. The first time I made the walk down Hagley Avenue and Lincoln Road, I heard fire sirens in the distance behind me. I turned and looked back. There was a huge cloud of smoke and the cacophony of many sirens. Later I heard that Ballantyne's shop had burned down, and there had been lives lost.

Auntie Margaret and Uncle Harold gave me a second home all the time I was living in Christchurch.

They had no family, and I determined then that if they should ever need it, I would give them a home. They later moved to Sherbourne Street and Auntie Margaret became ill and died in 1958.

Later, when Uncle Harold could no longer manage by himself, he came and lived with us for the rest of his life.

My sister Margaret [named after Auntie Margaret] helped Dad on the farm at home, working as a land girl. She met a boy from the city who was working on an [almost] adjacent farm. She came with him into town to meet his parents, and I was invited to come and have tea with them. During the evening their boarder came home, and I met Ken Love for the first time. When it was time for me to return to the hospital, I accepted his offer of a ride.

Three miles on the bar of a bike is a fairly memorable experience, but I accepted an invitation to go canoeing on the Avon the next Saturday.

Ken returned me to the nurses' old home and the next day I made my move to the new home. Our rooms [in both the old and new homes] were big enough to contain a single bed, a chair, a built in dressing table with drawers under it, and a wardrobe. Under the window was a steam heater connected to the hospital boiler, so we could adjust the heat and keep our rooms very comfortable.

There was another window on the inner wall facing the corridor, with a curtain that could be drawn across it. This curtain had to be left open at night, to allow the night supervisor to shine her torch in and ascertain that the occupant [and only the occupant] was present, and in bed. We had a disk that was to be hung on the outside of the door when we were on morning duty. The supervisor would then wake us at five, ready for our six o'clock shift.

Nurses' feet are notoriously tired and sore, and it became routine at bedtime to tuck the seat of our chair under the centre of the foot of the bed. This elevation made quite a difference.

The wards were long, and if one had something to take to the far end, it didn't pay to forget anything and have to make a second trip. "Nurse! When will you learn to use your head to save your feet?" From the ward where I did my junior night duty, to the nurses' dining room, was a quarter of a mile. At night time, the house surgeons would use bicycles in the corridors to go from ward to ward.

On the walls of my room I hung three pictures. They were all scenes—bluebells under silver birches—a thatched cottage in an English summer garden, and an autumn woodland scene. For one of my birthdays, my friends completed the seasons, with a picture of horses and sled between a cottage and a stream, in sunlit snow. These pictures moved with me from room to room.

As soon as I moved to the new home, I bought myself a second hand, treadle, Singer sewing machine. I now made myself a bedspread and curtains, and my room became quite distinctive. I also did a little dressmaking.

We usually had no difficulty sleeping, with shift work, lectures and swotting for imminent exams. In nursing circles, the best cure for insomnia was reputed to be, a good dose of 'Gowland and Cairney' [our anatomy and physiology textbook] taken at bedtime.

I did my operating theatre training over the December of my second year. Before we went to theatre Sister said "Now you are going to learn how to really clean! Next time you go home you are going to go into culture shock when you see how your Mother does her cleaning." She was right!!

I discovered that the two most difficult substances, of which to remove any trace, are plaster of Paris and blood.

After the most meticulous attention to every tiny smear, spots would still appear in the most unlikely places. Even a small spot of blood on the ceiling! I was able to remain upright during the first operation I attended; and thereafter, the only thing that I really had difficulty with, was the sound of metal chipping away at bone.

On Christmas day the theatre nurses and house surgeons spent the day in the theatre block, in case there were any emergencies. All remained quiet; and much of the day was passed with us all crowded into the office, some on chairs and some sitting on the floor, eating chocolate biscuits and taking it in turns to read aloud 'The Wind In the Willows'.

Busy Days

One week after moving to the new home, I came off morning duty and hurried to my room to change.

At two thirty, I descended the stairs to the vestibule inside the main door. One or two nurses were coming and going, and another was at the desk talking to the supervisor. There was no one else about.

I waited around for ten minutes or so, and then a very disappointed young nurse went slowly back up the stairs.

"Oh well, I might as well wash my hair." I undid my plaits, and was passing the phone on the way to the ablution block when the phone rang. Unusually, it was for me—I had a visitor down at the desk. With my hair around my shoulders I went down the stairs again.

It was a lovely afternoon and several canoes were on the river.

Although it was my first ride in a canoe, I managed not to overbalance, and we went quite a good distance upstream. Another canoe took to the river at the same time as us, and the very nervous female passenger put her hands on the bank.

The canoe moved out into the stream and a very wet girl scrambled up on to the bank.

During that afternoon Ken asked me two questions. "Would I like to go to the P and T ball with him?" And "was I doing anything next Saturday afternoon?"

During that week I paid a visit to a little dress shop on the corner of New Regent Street, where I had noticed that they had rather pretty garments in my size fourteen, at a very reasonable price.

I bought a sage green blouse to go with my brown tweed suit, and some red ribbon that might look all right as a bow at the neck.

The next Saturday afternoon we left the nurses' home soon after two thirty and took the tram to the foot of the Cashmere hills. We walked up to Victoria Park, and stayed there rather longer than we should have, as we had been invited to tea in Sydenham.

We ran down the hill and reached Albermarle Street only slightly late.

My nursing experience was extended with time spent in the ward with boys between five and twelve. I was not completely at ease there, and envied the girls who could relate naturally to these little lads. Little did I know that this was a training ground for when I would begin having my own family.

From there I progressed to isolation nursing, with short stints in men's urology and women's medical.

Somewhere along the way I did my senior night duty, but I can't remember where.

Three months flew by in accident and emergency. I particularly loved the work there.

On one memorable shift I was assisting a house surgeon who was about to suture a cut on a young man's arm. I tried to unscrew the cap of the bottle of local anaesthetic. I couldn't get it to budge and neither could the doctor. Then I had a brilliant idea; and holding the cap in the heel of the door, I screwed the bottle.

Off came the cap, and the neck of the bottle, slicing my finger in passing.

A very annoyed house surgeon put three sutures in the back of the base of my index finger [without anaesthetic], and then we returned to the poor patient, who had been witnessing all this drama. Five days later I took the sutures out of my own finger. I can still admire the scar.

Earlier in my training I had another experience in A and E. Under my arm became sore, and before long there was a large painful lump there. It was so painful that I decided to get it looked at in A and E.

I went there in the evening and sat in the waiting room in my uniform. There were several other patients there, and some of them were looking at me with very amused glances.

A Sister appeared and came over to me. "Do you realize that this is the STD clinic nurse"? I was none the wiser as I followed Sister into a side room.

She explained to me that the clinic for sexually transmitted diseases was probably not where I intended to be. She then called a house surgeon to look at my axilla, and he took me down to the operating theatre where the theatre staff were cleaning the theatres at the end of the day. In the midst of the mops and buckets, I was invited to hop up on to the table. I was given a few whiffs of anaesthetic, and when I came to, discovered that a large abscess had been opened and drained. I was told to return to A and E next day for a dressing.

I was officially off duty, sick; and my Ward Sister was advised. Next morning I had a message to report to another very busy ward, where they were short staffed.

I queried this order, but was told the situation was urgent, and I was to go.

I struggled into my uniform and [complete with arm in sling], I reported for duty. The Sister took one look at me and said; "You are no use to me like that Nurse!", so back I went to my room. It didn't take many days before I was fine and back on duty.

I spent three months nursing babies and young girls. The wee mites in huge frog plasters [for correction of congenital hips], were particularly appealing.

I was amazed at how happy most of them seemed to be, with a little love and attention.

One of the older girls had been in hospital for quite some time. She had rheumatic fever, and it was my job to give her medicine to her. She usually made a fuss about it, and one day she said; "Do you know how horrible this is Nurse?"

I realized that I didn't, and when I was out of her sight I tasted a tiny bit. It was probably not a good idea, because now I had not only her protests to deal with; but my sympathy as well!

During our second year there was a new introduction that made life so much easier.

The Study Day!—Instead of fitting in lectures around shifts; for each class there was now a whole day each week, just devoted to lectures and the academic part of our profession.

As we neared the end of our training we became senior nurses, with a second stripe on the sleeve, and part of our responsibilities was with training and encouraging our juniors.

One day as I was walking up the hill behind Cashmere, a couple of girls were following me, and they were close enough for me to clearly hear their conversation. One said, "I don't know if I should be nursing, so often I think, 'I've had enough of this, I think I'll leave.'"

I turned round and said to her "That's alright Nurse! We all feel like that at least once a day, but then there is so much that is rewarding, that one is always ready to carry on".

We had paused while we were talking, and an older woman who was behind us added "You are so right! I am a nurse too".

This and That

The position of the hospital boiler room was very obvious from a good distance away. The fifty five metre chimney towered high in the air. Hot water and steam were piped under the road, to and throughout, the hospital buildings and nurses' homes. Steam heated the sterilizers and the heaters in each ward and room.

Sterilisation of bedpans and urinals was the responsibility of the probationary nurses. The more senior nurses attended to instruments and syringes, plus needles for injections.

The glass syringes and assorted needles were flushed out and boiled. A staff nurse was responsible for the condition of the needles. They needed to be sharp, and of course without any trace of a barb. This was accomplished with fine sandpaper.

At the beginning of the era of Penicillin, it was hard on the patients, as the antibiotic was administered by intramuscular injection every four hours, day and night, into the buttock. However, it saved many lives.

"Turn over please!"

At mealtimes, only half of the staff left the ward at one time, so the patients were never left unattended. It was a very busy ward, and Sister and I were the only staff present. It became shambolic.

Everybody thought they needed attention right now, plus there was a genuine emergency.

We were just about run off our feet.

As the rest of the staff were returning there was no let up, and my seventeen years of farm training asserted itself as I said to Sister, "I am happy to work through, and get some tucker later." Sister looked horrified.

I'm sure if she hadn't been wearing her cap, her hair would have stood straight up on end.

"**Nurse**! **Horses** eat **tucker!** Nurses **dine!** Go and have your lunch immediately!"

Patients, who needed extra care, were often accommodated in a room with only two or three beds, close to the office. I opened the door and walked in. The sole occupant was lying on his back and had kicked off the covering bedclothes.

Suddenly a fountain arose from the centre of the bed, arched gracefully over and landed in the drinking glass on his locker.

I cleaned up the mess, changed the bed, re-covered the patient—again—and disposed of the glass.

I defy anyone to duplicate that effect intentionally.

After lunch bedpans were distributed and collected again.

The ward had been tidied, and patients were reclining comfortably on freshly shaken pillows; their hair combed and bed jackets covering their shoulders. The visitors were milling outside the closed ward door and the clock said one minute to two. On the way to open that door, I glanced at the bed nearest to it. On the floor was something brown – on closer inspection there was much more, and another handful followed before I had time to act.

I summoned some help, and then apologized to the visitors for the delay, before dealing with the situation.

Ken

At the end of May 1945 Ken turned fifteen and left school.

He immediately commenced working in the office at the Ellesmere Power Board. Office work is not Ken's thing; but he persevered and learned how to do the filing, address envelopes and run messages.

For six very long weeks he left home soon after eight fifteen a.m. with a cut lunch, and biked to Leeston. One day he forgot to take his lunch. The only thing available in the shop was some cold crumpets. Not being used to crumpets he ate them as they were, unadorned. He was not impressed.

On Friday the thirteenth of July, there was a northwest gale, and it was almost impossible to open the office door against it.

On the Saturday morning there was no electricity, and a foot of snow on the ground. Ken walked the mile in the snow, to see what was happening on the main street of Southbridge.

The linesmen, who were his workmates, were busy trying to restore power to the township. As soon as they saw him, the whole gang made a very thorough job of rolling him in the snow.

The weight of the snow on the lines would cause a line to snap. Without the support on that side of the pole, there was nothing to stop the poles on either side being pulled over. This created a domino effect, and there were areas where four miles of poles in a row, had been pulled over. These were mainly steel poles.

The linesmen worked long hours for many months, to restore power to the Ellesmere district. Ken was recruited from the office to help the linesmen. He did not receive any training, but learned as he acted as general rouseabout.

The inspector drove a V8 pick-up and Ken spent time assisting him.

They got stuck in a snowdrift in Springston, and in trying to extricate the pick-up, they managed to strip all the gears but top. There was certainly no reverse. As they inspected the poles in Leeston, Ken's job was to let the inspector out by a pole, then drive round the block and wait for him at the next pole back.

For the remainder of his six months working for the Power Board, Ken was with the linesmen. He then began an apprenticeship with a private electrical contractor. He loved the practical side of the work.

It was now necessary to board in Christchurch, and when he was returning to Southbridge for a weekend he usually caught the bus, but sometimes rode his pushbike. The return to the City was accomplished with the bike on the front of the bus.

As with most of his contemporaries, Ken obtained his driver's licence as soon as he turned fifteen. However he had never driven in the city.

Seated beside the Boss on the bench seat of the Essex car, he didn't know that that situation was soon to change. They crossed the bridge from Oxford Terrace into Victoria Street. The Boss was looking for a certain shop. Suddenly the car almost stopped, and the Boss said, "Here, you take over!" as he bailed out and disappeared into the shop. Ken slid behind the wheel and had to look for the nearest available parking spot.

They wired houses for a builder who worked over a very wide area. In the Boss's Willys work van, they were driving back from Reefton in the dark, and there was a slight detour to cross a bridge, about four miles before they reached Culverden.

They were travelling at about fifty miles per hour, and in the poor visibility, missed the detour and stopped suddenly, in the middle of a ford. Everything in the van was thrown forward, including Ken [there were no seatbelts then]. The motor didn't stop, and the only problem seemed to be the lights. There weren't any! In first gear they crawled out of the ford. Nothing to do but keep going!

A long time later they arrived back in Christchurch and stopped outside their shop. They noticed that the light switch [immediately in front of Ken] had been pushed in. They pulled it out into the on position.

Hey Presto! Lights!

Another time they had been working in Wataroa on the west coast. In the evening they came across Arthur's Pass and travelled back to Christchurch via Springfield at about seventy miles an hour. The next day they climbed into the van and set off for the first job.

Fifty yards down the road there was a massive bump, and a van wheel rolled past them and travelled a further fifty yards. The left back axle had broken!

An electrician spends a fair amount of time working above the ceiling of a house. At Governor's bay, in the middle of summer, the temperature climbed to ninety eight degrees *Fahrenheit*, and that was just outside.

In the ceiling cavity under a corrugated iron roof, an electrician and his apprentice spent much of the day wiring the electrical circuits.

It was unbelievably hot, and the perspiration poured from the pair. At the end of the day they both repaired to the nearby hotel. Ken drank seven, seven ounce glasses of lemonade before he could quench his thirst.

At one of the four different homes where he boarded during his apprenticeship, a fellow boarder worked in the evening, as a waiter at the Waldorf Nightclub.

He obtained a position for Ken there, and the tips earned from a few night's extra work, boosted his meagre income as an apprentice.

When he first started, apprentices received seventeen shillings and three pence per week. That equates to one dollar and seventy two cents. The true comparative value is shown by what that amount would buy.

A visit to the pictures cost nine pence, and for the same price we could buy sufficient fish and chips for one.

There were twenty shillings to one pound, and two pounds would buy a pair of shoes of average quality.

An accident with a tray of glasses was an embarrassing end to one evening.

Ken placed a full tray of empty wineglasses on a box on the bench, and proceeded to empty the tray.

He didn't allow for the overhang, and his next task was disposing of a rather large quantity of broken glass. Insurance must have covered the damage, because he wasn't penalized.

Each Saturday was spent picking up potatoes for one of the biggest market gardens in Marshlands. On two evenings per week there were polytech classes to attend, with the necessary swotting for tests. Somewhere among all these other activities, Ken fitted in Ballroom dancing classes. He had already earned a bronze medal by the time I met him.

I attended one class with him, but we didn't proceed any further.

One of Ken's Landladies served up some stewed fruit for dessert. It was not a fruit he recognized and he didn't enjoy it. Shortly afterwards he made a dash outside and was violently sick.

When we were first married he told me that he was allergic to tamarillos. As an experiment, I included a minute amount of tamarillo in some stewed apple—not even enough to taste. It only took a matter of minutes to prove he was right.

The usual early morning wake-up call; up and dressed; a nice plate of hot porridge with sugar and milk, washed down with a cup of tea; pick up the lunch bag and off to work.

Cycle across town—not much traffic about this morning!

Arrive at work to find door locked.

Look at watch. How will I fill this hour until everyone else arrives?

Ken's Father was an Agricultural Contractor. He lived in Southbridge and owned a few acres of land down by the beach.

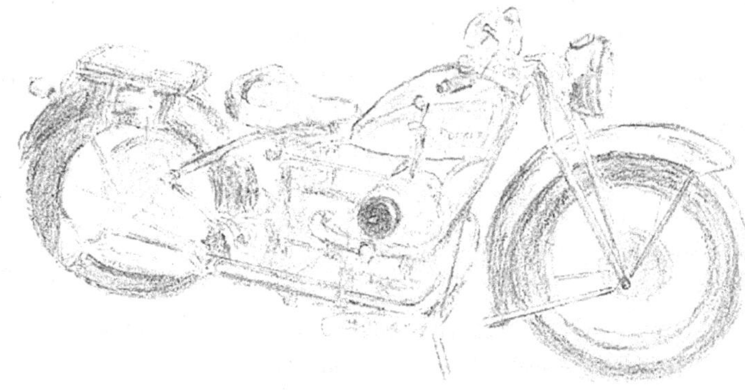

To attend to his sheep he would ride his Douglas Twin motorbike between properties. By 1948 Ken had saved enough money to purchase this motorbike from his Father.

It was one thing to own a motorbike, and quite another to have enough money for the petrol to run it. By the time I met him; he had made one trip to Dunedin to visit his Grandparents. He usually only used it to travel out to Southbridge and back. For any travel in the City the bicycle sufficed.

On the way back from Dunedin, he was lucky that the blowout he had; was in the township of Rakaia.

At this time post war, there was still a shortage of tyres, but the garage did have a roll of insulation tape. A quick wrap up and he was on his way again back to Southbridge.

Dougall, [Ken's brother] rode an Indian Scout motorbike and for the 1948 Christmas holidays, the two brothers had planned a motorcycle tour of the west coast.

As a Scout Leader, Dougall's camp planning would have not omitted any important items.

They set out from Southbridge and got to within two miles of Springfield before the Indian broke down. Ken towed him with the Douglas to the nearest garage.

It was an exceedingly hot day, and they stopped at the nearby hotel for a drink. Dougall ordered a sarsaparilla and Ken; a lemonade. The barman looked at him and said, "That's a b....y silly drink!" He didn't charge Ken for it.

They crossed the road to the garage, and the proprietor invited them to take the bikes into the back of the garage, strip the Indian down, and work on it as late as they wished. They discovered a broken piston. They blew up their Lilos, and settled into their sleeping bags on the floor of the garage. Next morning they caught the railcar to Christchurch, bought the parts they required from a second hand shop, and returned to Springfield on the afternoon railcar.

By one o'clock in the morning the bike was ready for the road, and they spent a second night on the garage floor. In the morning they were on their way again.

Four years later when Ken stopped at that garage for some petrol, the proprietor handed him a spanner and said. "This is the spanner you boys left behind after working on your motorbike."

There were no more mechanical problems, and they crossed Arthur's Pass and continued up the west coast where an absolute deluge of rain caused them to seek shelter in a barn by the roadside. It was fairly short lived, and they travelled on via the Buller gorge to Nelson, and then across to Blenheim.

Dougall had his pilot's licence; so they hired a Tiger Moth and flew across the strait to Wellington. After staying the night with their aunt, they flew back to Blenheim. The hire of the plane plus hanger fees was five pounds.

Aromas

ON OUR FIRST DAY IN preliminary school, one of our lectures and discussions dealt very fully with personal hygiene.

"Your patients have enough to deal with, without having to put up with any unnecessary unpleasantness from their nurse!"

Nearly all the female patients appeared to have the same preference for toilet soap; and nearly all the nurses couldn't bear it. I think it must have reacted chemically with some of the other smells we were putting up with.

We always referred to it among ourselves by a parody of its brand name.

I didn't meet up with any brand of talcum powder that I definitely didn't like.

Some of the smells had to be quickly dealt with for everybody's wellbeing. Burning blue gum leaves in a room banished much unpleasantness. I have since learned that even striking a match will burn off some odorous gasses from the air.

Dry mustard rubbed on ones hands, dealt with some particularly clinging smells.

In most wards there was always the smell of fresh flowers—brightening the day for the staff as well as the patients. At night these migrated to the corridor or any other area away from the patients; and these areas would now smell like a florist shop.

A morning job was to change the water if necessary, and return them to their rightful owners. One of the more objectionable aromas; is that of stale water in a vase.

A task after visitors had departed; was to put any gifts of flowers into vases; and at the other end of the scale, was the disposal of those past their best.

I enjoyed the smell of winter green and most other embrocations. Some of the nurses became over fond of the smell of the anaesthetics, and couldn't resist taking the odd whiff when cleaning the theatres.

Many years later, as I was cleaning some stainless steel with methylated spirits, someone said to me, "this place smells like a hospital."

We must have been doing something right, if the only smell reminiscent of a hospital was Meths!

My handwriting could never have been described as Copperplate! In fact that word should not have been used in the same sentence as my hand writing. However it was readable.

All of our lectures had to be transcribed into an exercise book as they were being delivered—if we wanted to be able to study and revise them. I developed a scrawl that probably only I could read.

When an orderly delivered any item for a patient to the ward, he required a signature on the delivery slip, from the nurse to whom he entrusted that item.

The flowers were lovely, and I held them in one hand while I signed the slip with the other. The orderly looked at the slip and said, "Should I take this to the dispensary and have it made up?"

Originally doctors' prescriptions and signatures were notorious for being illegible—probably for the same reason.

Later, I realized that my difficulties were minor compared to those of another nurse.

She was Asian, and still at that stage with the English language, where she had to mentally translate everything into her own tongue, before she could fully understand it.

Christmas

BEFORE EACH CHRISTMAS THE NURSES had a few practice sessions, to make sure we were all familiar with the well-known Christmas carols, and could sing them in unison.

On Christmas Eve a long line, comprising all off duty nurses [in uniform] plus any nurses who could be spared from the wards, assembled in the corridor. With each nurse carrying a lighted candle, we started to sing and wended our way through all the wards.

Most of the patients loved it, though I hate to think how much time lapse there was, between the singers at each end of the line.

A minimum number of patients remained in hospital on Christmas Day. Anyone well enough was allowed home. There were no nurses having a day off.

We were there to make the day as enjoyable as possible for our patients. Of course these were the most unwell patients anyway. During the morning the Medical and Surgical Specialists would pay a social call and greet all their patients. There were usually a few chocolates etc. for the staff!

Part way through the year was the nurses' fancy dress party and concert. A strictly female only occasion! The costumes and skits were heavily weighted with a hospital bias. With regard to one costume, Matron was heard to remark, "Isn't she cold?"

A very nice supper was served, and the light hearted revelry was a very pleasant interlude.

The annual Nurses' Ball was a very formal affair held at the Winter Gardens in Gloucester Street.

My second Ball was just after I met Ken, and I had already invited a boy I knew from Waipara dancing days.

Ken had already invited me to the Post and Telegraph Ball; and for that I splashed out and bought myself a blue and pink floral evening dress. I could only afford a small splash! But it was quite pretty! Ken had been given the tickets for this occasion.

About this time I invited Ken to come up to Manahune and meet the rest of the Thomson Clan. The next time I had a day off during the weekend, I experienced travel as pillion passenger on a motor bike. Dressed in jumper and skirt, with a warm woollen coat, lisle stockings and strong walking shoes; I didn't look the part; but this would continue to be my motorcycling costume for the next five years.

Ken wore a close fitting, leather cap, and I would sometimes wear a beret.

We never wore crash helmets—and neither did any other cyclist; except on the race track! A change of clothing travelled in backpacks while we were using the Douglas motor bike.

Stan, who was Margaret's fiancé, had an Ariel bike, and my brother Bert, a Royal Enfield.

With six of us on the motor bikes [our brother John was with Bert], and the youngest [Harold] plus a bountiful picnic lunch, in the Austin Seven with Mum and Dad, we went to the Leithfield Beach for the day.

In those days Leithfield had a beautiful sandy beach, with not a trace of shingle. One could dig up pipis in the wet sand, to take home for the evening meal.

I received an invitation for myself and a partner, to attend a twenty first birthday dance in the Ellesmere district. Ken's parents invited me to spend the night after the dance at their home. We arrived there on the Douglas and had tea.

We were intending to go to the dance the same way, but Ken's father offered him the use of his wee Rover, so we went in style.

For their first twenty years of marriage Ken's parents only had one car.

This was a blue two-seater Rover. The top was black canvas and incorporated side windows of celluloid. The boot opened up to disclose a dicky-seat. This was neatly upholstered the same as inside. From it, there was an abundance of fresh air and a wonderful view of the back of the cab. The car was started with a crank handle, and had a brass worm-drive tail shaft. It was a very reliable little car.

One day while they were living at Tipirita there was a flood. In the Rover his dad approached the Selwyn River; only to discover a line of bigger, newer vehicles reluctant to ford the river. After assessing the situation he drove a short distance upstream, then into the river on an angle.

The spectators looked on in amazement as the cheeky little car drove out of the river on the opposite side, and disappeared down the road.

When their two little lads were about seven and three respectively, they drove to Dunedin to visit the boys' grandparents. The boot was filled with luggage; Dougall sat between his parents, and

Ken was enthroned on a block of firewood placed on the floor between his mother's legs. I don't know who to be most sorry for, Mother or Son?

When Ken first took me to Southbridge, his parents were still revelling in their green Singer sedan, and the Rover had been relegated to work vehicle.

Days Off

On one or two occasions Lenore was able to accompany me for a night and day at Manahune.

On one of these occasions she suggested that a no [read BAD] manners meal would be fun.

Mum and Dad were rather horrified at first. After all—they had spent many years trying to train their brood to the stage where they could safely be let loose in polite society. However, they relaxed, and were finally able to [almost] enter into the spirit of the occasion.

I don't think that that was the time when a fully creamed meringue spattered on the wall, close to the head of a very cheeky brother.

A day off during the week was sometimes spent with Auntie Margaret.

Her brother had helped them build their own home. It was a cosy little cottage, set facing the sun, in the centre of one side of their section. The entry was into the kitchen in the centre of the building. The bathroom was adjacent, and the door to the bedroom also opened into the kitchen, beside the bathroom. On the opposite side was a spacious, comfortable lounge, well equipped with book shelves.

A garage for their Citroen car, with an attached workshop for Uncle Harold's numerous carpentry projects, was on the other side of the section. A well-kept garden supplied most of their vegetables and fruit—I first became acquainted with feijoas there. A pretty little stream formed the back boundary, and, with a bit of ingenious piping, they also had a tiny adjacent lily and goldfish pond, surrounded by arum lilies, Japanese iris and astilbes.

One day Auntie Margaret was quite upset because an enterprising heron had just had her goldfish for lunch.

Thereafter, the pond was kept covered with wire-mesh.

The Botanical gardens were a convenient place for a little exercise in the sun.

In spring, the glades of daffodils drew many visitors, and I suspect that the uniformed nurses wandering there added to the attraction.

One of my rambles took me to the rose gardens, where I joined a group surrounding a gardener who was deadheading roses. She explained how to always make one's cut just above a leaf with at least five leaflets [where a strong bud would probably already be making its appearance] and there would soon be the growth for a second flowering. I have always followed her advice, and have passed on the tip to many others.

When I had my bicycle, I used it to go into the centre of town. There were bicycle stands at frequent intervals among the parking spots. Each stand would hold about ten bicycles parallel parked, with the front wheel between two uprights. It was necessary to padlock the bike to the stand.

Ken and I made one bicycle expedition together. From the hospital we biked to TaiTapu, and then back to Christchurch along a narrow shingle road close beside the Port hills.

On either side of the road, there were high hawthorn hedges, and I thought it was probably quite similar to an English country lane—lovely.

Care was necessary when one was biking parallel to tram tracks. If the front wheel dropped into the groove, it almost certainly meant a tumble. It was also advisable to be alert when following a tram, as it would veer to the left at the tram passing bays.

On Riccarton Road, Ken saw the front bogie wheels of a tram veer left, and a malfunction of the points caused the rear bogie to veer right. The tram was now at an angle to the thoroughfare, in the middle of Riccarton road.

The conductor jumped out and readjusted the power contact arms at each end of the tram.

The tram backed up and the conductor readjusted the points. He switched contact arms again and there were no more problems.

Trams were the main means of public transport in the city. At peak hours all the seats would be full, and the centre aisle packed with standing passengers, all holding on to leather straps suspended from a rail just under the roof. Everyone would be swaying as the tram turned the corners.

When we first moved into the nurses' old home, our bedrooms were close to hospital corner, facing onto Riccarton Avenue. The trams would rattle and bang day and night, as they came round the corner. We thought we would never sleep again! It only took two or three days before we hardly noticed them.

Hagley Park

When Ken and I started going out on a regular basis, we didn't have any money to spare, so we went walking.

When I had a morning duty, on one evening during the week he would bicycle to the nurses' home after tea, and we would go for a walk.

Quite often we crossed the Antigua street foot bridge and walked along Rolleston Avenue. In the summer, if the botanical gardens were still open, that is where we would go. If the gates were shut, our route would probably lead across the Armagh street bridge. We would then follow the river round, back to the hospital. In other words, we walked round the block—quite a large block.

All student nurses had to be back in the home by ten pm. Then the gates would be locked.

Occasional late night passes were available. It was common knowledge that there was a loose rod in the fence, and that a little negotiation with a friend whose room was on the ground floor, could lead to access via a window. I never bothered to find out more about it, as both Ken and I were more in need of our sleep.

Nurses' breakfast was served at eight am. Even if I was on morning duty, I would make sure that I reached the home in time to run up the stairs to the first floor ablution block, open the window, and be ready to wave as a familiar figure cycled past on his way to work. We very rarely missed that morning ritual.

Dad had never been interested in alcohol. Both he and Mum were happy to drink a very small Port wine or Sherry on a special celebration. However there had been one occasion on which Dad admitted that he had been drunk. He and his brother had worked all day in the hot sun, splitting logs at the Glenmark Homestead. As they were leaving at the end of the day, they passed a tree of fully ripe peaches. Most of these were lying in the grass under the tree and they gave in to temptation.

They sat beside the tree and quenched their thirst with luscious, warm, juicy peaches.

They stood up and mounted their push bikes to begin their three and a half mile ride home. The peaches had started to ferment in the hot sun and were very alcoholic. This, they only realized, as they began to weave an extremely wavering course along the road.

When I was sixteen, I was staying with a friend just prior to Christmas.

With her parents we went next door to visit their elderly neighbours. These very hospitable folk produced a bottle of their home made elderberry wine, and poured me a large glass. The colour was the same as sunshine through red stained glass, and it tasted lovely. They said farewell on their front steps, and we started down the long straight concrete path to the front gate.

I think I travelled about three times as far as I did on our arrival.

I could never understand why some nice boys found it necessary to drink to excess at dances. Their antics and inability to even remain on their feet, I found extremely off-putting, and I had decided early in my life, that I would not be marrying anyone who was a drinker. Another decision was the determination to not kiss anyone except my husband.

Ken's parents were not interested in alcohol either.

Ken did not like the taste of beer and saw no reason to drink it. When a group of his contemporaries told him that it 'took a man to drink', he replied, "It takes a better man not to!"

My parents had never been smokers; although Dad's brother had smoked a pipe, and his father had smoked to excess.

About half of the nurses smoked. For most of them; I did not think it did anything for them visually, but one girl managed to look extremely elegant with her cigarette in her hand.

As far as I was concerned, my money had been too hard-earned, to see it go up in smoke. I always said I was too mean to smoke!

In the hospital museum we were shown a smoker's lung. It was black and looked revolting. Shortly after that, I helped to nurse a patient who was dying of lung cancer. He was still smoking!

I was very relieved that neither I, nor other members of my family were smokers.

Ken's father was a light smoker and Ken was not particularly interested, but would have the odd cigarette. I only remember seeing him smoke once, and although we never discussed smoking, that was his last cigarette.

Milford Track

Auntie Margaret and Uncle Harold were very interested in New Zealand's flora and fauna, and had walked many of the popular bush tracks. Several times I heard them aver that Milford Sound was the climax of New Zealand scenery.

At that stage the only road access to the sound was the Milford track. The Homer tunnel was still under construction.

My annual holiday was imminent, and I had an idea. Next visit home, I asked Dad and Mum whether they would like to walk the Milford track with me. Dad's reply was entirely predictable. He loved Manahune, and whenever he was away, he was breaking his neck to get back there. He was 'much too busy'. I could see that Mum was interested, and with the rest of the family we wore down the objections.

Dad was very fit, and Mum was anything but! Mum started immediately walking back and forth, up and down the hills between the house and wool shed. I made the necessary reservations.

Mum had another concern. She didn't want her sons to miss out, so she contacted a cousin who had a holiday home at the New Brighton beach, and arranged the use of it for a week. She took the boys there for a week at the seaside, before she and Dad left for their holiday.

They were returning home on the Sunday, and Ken and I rode there on the Douglas, to spend the afternoon with them and help them pack up. We were left to lock up and return the key. When we were on our own Ken plucked up all his courage and asked." Will you marry me?" The answer was a very emphatic "YES."

A while later we noticed that it had started to rain—in fact it was pouring down.

Lock up and return the key—then the ride back to the city. We were following a tram, and when it stopped to pick up a passenger, Ken pulled up beside it and I boarded too.

Ken passed us, and then we passed him—stopped on the side of the road. This scenario was repeated numerous times before we reached the Square.

As the rain had eased a little, I completed the journey on the back of the bike. The rain had been wetting the spark plug, and he had to keep drying it before the motor would start.

We said 'Goodbye' in the rain, and it was nearly two weeks before we were together again.

I was now on holiday; and the next day, Dad, Mum and I travelled by bus to Te Anau. We spent a night in the lake side hotel; then there was a morning's ride on the launch to Glade House at the head of the lake.

After a picnic lunch beside the water with our guide, we were walking the Milford track.

The walkers crossed a swing bridge, but the guide was leading a pack horse laden with supplies for the first hut, so his route was through the Clinton River.

The first afternoon's walk was an easy ten mile walk on a wide path, that led through moss and lichen covered bush. It was an idyllic April afternoon, our packs were not too heavy —we didn't have to carry food—and we arrived at the hut ready for our evening meal, which was soon set before us.

The second day started out fine. Dad had his own, plus Mum's gear in his pack. Mum was finding it progressively more difficult as we ascended to the McKinnon Pass, so Dad and I took turns taking her hand and giving her a tow.

By the time we reached the top it was misty and beginning to rain, so we didn't wait around long. It was a rather damp afternoon but Mum managed quite well on the descent.

The Quinton Hut provided a very nice meal and a good night's sleep. For those who wished to rise early, there was the opportunity to make a quick visit to the Sutherland Falls before breakfast.

After breakfast we were on our way for the final thirteen miles to Sandfly Point. It had rained hard over night and every slope seemed to have its own waterfall. The final three miles skirted the shores of Lake Ada. From Sandfly Point, it was only a short boat trip, and we were there.

We were accommodated in the Annex at the Mitre peak Lodge, and revelled in a hot shower and a change of clothing before tea.

Next morning, the sun was shining as we were taken on a cruise around Milford Sound.

The abundance of rain was now providing us with magnificent waterfalls everywhere. The Bowen falls were at their very best, and Mitre Peak lived up to its reputation for grandeur, on this sunny morning.

At the entrance to the sound, the Tasman Sea provided rather more tossing than I was comfortable with, but we were soon back into smoother waters.

A bus transported us to the Milford end of the Homer Tunnel. We disembarked, and with pack on back, and torch in hand, set out on our next adventure.

There was an abundance of rubble on the floor, and water streamed down the walls, before most of it was run away in a depression beside the wall. The only sign of 'men at work' was the odd shovel, and some random pieces of machinery that showed up occasionally in the beam of the torch.

After a long, eerie, uphill trek, we emerged into the sunshine and climbed on board the waiting bus.

Next stop—Queenstown.

Autumn in Queenstown provided colours we had never seen in Canterbury. There was red everywhere. Our accommodation was rather cold, and we went to bed early to keep warm. Next day it was up early to catch the bus for home.

For months Dad excitedly talked about the Milford Track, and anyone could have been forgiven for thinking that it was all his idea!

Mum and Dad were both fifty four when they did that walk.

Over fifty years later, Mum would still smile when we mentioned it, and say, "I DID IT."

Engaged

Whenn we had returned to Manahune after our walk, I spent the second week of my holiday there and Ken came up on the Douglas on the Saturday. Very nervously he sought out Dad, who was busy killing a sheep.

Very soon after, a very jubilant Ken came into the kitchen, and we announced to the rest of the family that we were engaged. On Sunday evening we both returned to Christchurch by motor bike.

The following Friday evening we were both free, so we visited a jeweller, and I left his shop wearing an engagement ring. When I was on duty the ring was still with me, in my pocket.

Since we started our training, the old Saint Andrew's manse had been pulled down; and a new single story building now replaced it.

The hospital had expanded its outpatients' department with the Saint Andrew's clinic, on Tuam Street. This clinic was staffed by a Sister and one nurse.

On my return from holiday I was posted as clinic nurse. This position had its own timetable. On Monday, Tuesday, Wednesday and Friday I worked from eight thirty am to four thirty pm. Thursday was my study day, and on Saturday I worked from six am until two pm in A and E.

My day off was Saturday afternoon through to Sunday evening for the next three months. Unheard of!!

For most of those days off Ken and I went alternately to Southbridge and Manahune.

At eight thirty I would arrive at the clinic and sterilize any equipment required for that day, before setting up the necessary instrument trays and preparing the surgeries and examination rooms.

I would be kept busy for the rest of the day, attending to the welfare of the patients, occasionally assisting a doctor, and the preparation of morning tea for the staff. Then there was the final clean up and tidying of the clinic at the end of the day.

It was Nurses' Ball time again; and this time I was able to wear the pretty, pale blue, bridesmaid's dress I had worn for Margaret and Stan's wedding the previous year. On that special occasion, Ken had been in the wedding entourage also, as groomsman.

The Douglas motorbike was now getting a lot of use, and was a bit unreliable, so Ken decided to trade it in, as a deposit on a new Triumph 500 Speed Twin. Rather than having him spend extra for time payment, I decided to help him out with the small amount necessary to make it freehold. There were saddle bags [so no more backpacks] and one of the greatest blessings, for Ken, was the wind shield.

The only close call we had was when returning from Akaroa. We hit an area of deep shingle and it was a bit scary for a few moments.

Apparently the mode of travel had been noted.

A house surgeon, who I didn't know, came into my ward and said "Oh, you're the nurse who rides around on the back of a motorbike!"

Finals

ON MAY TWENTY SECOND WE sat our hospital final exam, and in another fortnight it was the time for the State Finals.

During the nerve-racking wait for the results, we had a class photo taken on the steps of the nurses' home. Finally a large group of girls gathered in trepidation around the home notice board. For most it was a joyful outcome, but a few were disappointed.

Those nurses, who were going to continue working at the hospital, were now staff nurses and donned a blue uniform.

While nursing I had two attacks of acute abdominal pain that required admission as a patient. Both times it settled down without intervention, and was diagnosed as a grumbling appendix.

The first time coincided with my twenty first birthday. When I was well enough to next visit Auntie Margaret, she gave me a beautifully decorated birthday cake that she had had specially made for my twenty first. The second time was even more untimely.

Although I was being discharged that evening, they [the-powers-that-be] decreed that I was not permitted to attend any functions. As I passed the dining room on the way to my room, I paused for a few minutes, looking through the glass doors into the area where Mum, Dad and Ken were attending my graduation, on my behalf.

After the ceremony was over, I was able to spend a little time with them in the nurses' lounge.

Over the next few weeks the city photographers were inundated with uniformed nurses wearing shiny new medals.

Staff Nurse

THE CLEAN LAUNDRY WAS RETURNED to the wards in large, lidded wicker baskets that ran on castors. The staff nurse was responsible for the linen cupboard, as one of her duties. I took a pride in the appearance of 'my' cupboard [which was really a small room]. The baskets were unloaded onto the shelves running round the walls.

Just a few years ago, an ex-nurse who had been one of my juniors, told me that she used to be scared to take anything out of that cupboard—in case she left anything out of place. 'Was that a good thing or a bad thing?'

Without the need to study, I now had time for hand crafts. I knitted myself a two ply, teal, lacy jumper, and I bought the rug wool and canvas for a floor mat. I designed it myself, with a pattern of autumn leaves on a green background.

The mat took about six months to finish. I used it continuously for fifty years before I gave it to somebody else, to use in their caravan.

After I had been a staff nurse for five months, Dad told me that he knew of somebody who was looking for a full time nurse for a cerebral palsy patient. "Would I be interested?"

I knew that my nursing career was for a limited period of time, and I decided to take up the challenge.

After I had resigned, I heard that I had been about to be offered a permanent post in A and E. If that had already happened, it would have made my decision making much harder.

I purchased some uniforms. [I could only find white ones so I dyed them blue.] A week later I began my five months of nursing a private patient.

I had an hour for rest in the afternoon, as there was some night work involved.

I was free in the evenings from seven o'clock, and I had Saturday night and Sunday off.

It was a very nice family. The mother was a very good cook and gardener, and I made the most of my opportunities for some free tuition in these skills. When I finally left, she took me round her garden and gave me some very choice plants. Some of these have made all the shifts that I have, and have special memories for me.

For the rest of the year, Ken and I were able to spend almost the same amount of time together as we had before. There was no longer a morning wave from the nurses' home window!

Ken finished his apprenticeship at the end of the year, and his brother, Dougall, invited him to join his workforce as a builder.

Dougall had a small workshop behind their parents' house. Both sons now lived at home, and had about forty yards to travel to work.

Dougall and Zita were married in January, and Ken was their groomsman.

Soon after Christmas my employers told me that before they employed me, they had advertised overseas for an older woman to care permanently for their son. They had now had an application for the position, and they would be very grateful if I would continue to care for him, until my replacement arrived at the end of February.

Of course they knew that I was engaged, and sooner or later would be leaving to marry.

Near the end of February, I had very severe side and back pain and was diagnosed with a severe kidney infection. I was too ill to work anyway, but was able to overlap with the next nurse and introduce her to the intricacies of the position.

Glory Box

As a surprise for me for Christmas, Ken had commissioned Dougall to make a glory-box. It was beautifully made, and finished with an oak veneer. The hollow lid was rounded at the front and hinged to the main box. It was prevented from opening too far by two brass chains. A removable tray kept smaller items together.

The top of the lid was inlaid with several contrasting woods, and it was by far the loveliest piece of furniture we have ever owned. It *was* delivered to Manahune and was waiting for me when I returned home.

I spent a while just recuperating, and then was just happy to assist Mum as required, and work around the orchard and garden.

The post office must have prospered, because there was a vast increase in the flow of mail between Waipara and Southbridge.

Dougall and Zita took us with them for a weekend's deer-stalking, by the Leader River. Not a deer in sight, but a pleasant camping experience.

At Easter we flew to Dunedin to visit Ken's Grandparents, and returned to Christchurch by rail. Ken had had severe earache during the flight, so he was glad of this option.

Ken came to Manahune for an occasional week end.

About the middle of May he made one of these visits, and he had something to ask. A house in Southbridge was soon becoming available, and how would it be if we were to get married and move in? We discussed time frames with Mum and Dad, and it was all on!

If we were going to be paying rent, we might as well be living in the house. It was going to take six weeks to get a marriage licence—could we get everything else together in that time?

Church and Vicar—Glenmark of course, where Dad and Mum had been married twenty five years previously.

Bride's maid and Best man—Ken's Cousin Jean and my Brother Bert.

Caterer—Our favourite only available on the Friday—We could run with that. Reception—at the Waipara hall.

Invitations—send out as soon as possible.

Dress—The one made for Margaret using the figured satin from Mum's wedding dress. Just a few minor adjustments were necessary.

Going Away Costume—A few fittings at a Christchurch tailors, and he produced a very smart blue-grey suit of skirt and jacket to be worn with a new white blouse.

Ken's Twenty first—A few days too late; so his Father's permission and signature were needed for the marriage certificate.

Furniture—We acquired minimum of necessary second hand items.

Flowers—Ring the florist.

Banns—read in Church on the last three Sundays before the wedding. At least there were no objections!

Kitchen evening—A dance organized by the district, for local girls before their weddings. Admission was a gift for the bride's kitchen.

Meetings with the Vicar—two or three.

Wedding cake—made by mum and iced by Zita, who stayed at Manahune for two days before the wedding. I was privileged to be able to watch all the stages of this specialist work. There was much intricate piping involved. As I watched I thought "I could do that!" and a seed was sown!

Wedding ring—organized by Ken.

All sorts of other behind the scenes jobs—noted and attended to, by our caring family and friends.

Married

ON THE THURSDAY EVENING KEN went to Margaret and Stan's home to spend the night.

Friday morning was a bit of a blur, but after an early lunch it was time to get ready and put on *the dress*. Dad drove me to the church in the Austin seven. There we were met by the photographer whose record of the day has kept it fresh over the years.

Dad escorted me up the aisle of the beautifully decorated church, filled with our family and friends, to where a very nervous Ken was waiting.

We managed to make all our responses audibly, and then it was time to sign the register and certificate in the vestry.

Back in the church, the vicar introduced Mr. and Mrs. Ken Love, and to the majestic strains of the wedding march played on the organ, we made our way slowly down the aisle. As we neared the door a joyful peal of bells rang out, as the bell ringer added this special embellishment to our day.

There was a pause on the steps for photos, and then we posed for the more formal ones on the church lawn with a backdrop of trees.

The decorated hall bore witness to what had been occupying quite a number of people, and the caterers presented a meal that was up to their usual high standard.

In the evening there was a dance to which the whole district had been invited. We danced to the stimulating music of piano and two saxophones.

As usual the musicians appeared to be tireless. Just before supper I disappeared for a short time and changed into my going-away costume. We had another dance and then a neighbour drove us to his garage where he had allowed Ken to park our vehicle; hopefully out of the range of mischievous brothers.

For our honeymoon Ken had hired a small Bradford van, and we drove to a reserve at the base of the Port hills, where we camped overnight. In the morning we had breakfast with Auntie Margaret and Uncle Harold before driving to Dunedin. We had already discovered that our luggage now contained rather a large amount of confetti.

Ken's Grandparents had loaned us their home for a fortnight while they stayed up in Southbridge.

This allowed us to holiday very comfortably and cheaply, and Ken was able to introduce me to some of the haunts of his childhood years.

We returned on the Thursday; calling in to our new home to unload the van before driving to Christchurch. After spending the night in a hotel, we returned the van and picked up Ken's Triumph, before riding back to Southbridge.

This time we were going home.

Home

Towards the end of the nineteenth century, many suburban and semi-rural dwellings were of an adapted villa construction. Outwardly they were a square box shape with a hip roof. There were concrete foundations and the piles were square quarried stones that supported the floor joists, but were unattached. The house sat squarely in the centre of the section. On the side facing the road there was a central front door flanked by two sash windows.

From the front door, a central hallway led to the door in the centre of the house, opening into the kitchen-living room. On either side of the front door, a door opened into a room off the hall. One would be a bedroom, and the other room, adjacent to the kitchen, would be used as a sitting room. A shared chimney catered for an open fire place in the sitting room, and a coal range in the kitchen. From the kitchen there was a door opening to a second bedroom. Sash windows on either side of the house, catered for the kitchen and bedroom, respectively.

A lean-to on the back of the house served as an entry porch and scullery. There was a bench with a shelf beneath, under a casement window, and an outside door at the end. Behind this door were hooks for coats and hats.

The walls of the main living area were lined with varnished match lining. The rest of the walls–plus the ceilings–had laths covered with hessian scrim and wallpaper.

Between the coal range and the outside wall was a floor to ceiling built in cupboard, accessed by four hinged doors. This cupboard doubled as pantry and china cabinet.

Outside the back door, a path of uneven slabs of broken concrete, led to the corrugated iron, dirt floored wash house. This housed copper and double wooden tubs, with a hand turned, roller clothes wringer between the two tubs. There was sufficient area to store a small supply of dry firewood for house and laundry.

Opposite the laundry door was the supply of water for the section. The hand pump was always available to fill buckets of beautiful water for use in the house or wash house. Hot water was available from the large kettle always simmering on the coal range, or if larger quantities were required for baths or laundry, it was necessary to heat it in the copper.

The time it was most appreciated was on a hot summer's day as a refreshing cold drink.

Washing up was done in a basin on the scullery bench, and the water was then thrown on the garden. Washing of face and hands was accomplished the same way. For a bath, the portable tin bath could be used in the wash house, close to the hot water supply, or especially for the children, in front of the coal range. Whichever position was adopted, it was still necessary to dispose of the waste water before hanging the bath back in the wash house.

A visit to the toilet was always preceded by a stroll in the fresh air—along the path in front of the wash house—around beside the curved willow hedge that enclosed the coal heap, and there it was; a neat little house, that contained a hinged bench seat with a circular hole, over a large metal straight-sided bucket, complete with wire handle.

To one side of the seat sat a box full of newspaper squares, and a tall shaker-top tin of disinfecting and deodorizing powder.

The hole was always kept covered with a lid to discourage flies. At least once a week the man of the house would indulge in a little extra exercise, digging a hole behind the olearia hedge and emptying the bucket.

To a house of this description, Ken's father brought his wife and two sons early in the nineteen thirties. They were also able to lease the five acres of land surrounding the house. On this land there was a shed where he housed his Rover car and tractor. The land was divided into two paddocks. One was used for cropping, and in the other he grazed a house cow. On some land nearer the coast he ran a flock of sheep. His main occupation was as an agricultural contractor.

The boys had plenty of space to play, and later spent many happy hours by the little creek that traversed the land.

After the hard years during the depression, life gradually became a little easier and Ken's parents were able to buy a block of land, and finally to build themselves a home there.

It became feasible to invest in a Sunshine header harvester, and so his father would be occupied in the off season, he had a gorse cutter specially made. During the school holidays when he was fourteen, Ken worked on the header, sewing bags of wheat, and heaving them about.

When I first visited them, Ken's mother had a lovely flower garden, and a very productive vegetable garden and orchard. I am sure that similar would have been the case at their previous home.

In the July of nineteen fifty one, this was the house that had again become available.

There were some differences. On the roof of the lean-to there was a one hundred gallon water tank.

This had a float gauge with a weight on the outside of the tank. If the weight was near the top of the tank it was time to turn on the electric pump in the cupboard under the sink. The lean-to had been extended with a bathroom, and a small electric cylinder in the bathroom supplied hot water to bath, hand basin and sink. Cold water had been piped to the wash house, and the grey water from all these facilities was drained away.

We moved into a house—now to make it into a home!

Settling In

IT DIDN'T TAKE LONG TO arrange our furniture.

In the kitchen there was a large wooden kitchen table, with cutlery drawer incorporated, plus two wooden kitchen chairs.

Under the window we placed an old sofa that had a padded seat and wooden back. In front of the coal range was a rag mat that in the far distant past, had been lovingly handmade, probably by another young bride.

In the corner beside the sofa Ken made a shelf to hold our secondhand radio, and between the door and the table, we placed a butter box as a small utility shelf and cupboard. This could also double as an extra chair.

The bedroom contained an old oak double bed and dressing table [that had been inherited from Ken's Love grandparents] my hooked mat and glory-box. There was also a small, not very comfortable, new armchair, that I had purchased without sitting in it first, [lesson learnt]! One room we left empty, and in the other stored some boxes of books and a collection of butter boxes and twenty pound fruit cases that we had been accumulating. My sewing machine lived in this room too.

Our crockery and cutlery were an interesting collection of very old and very new.

With Mum's blessing, I had helped tidy her cutlery drawer by removing a few items well past their best, that I knew she never used. When intermingled with shiny new [wedding present] dessert, tea and serving spoons, they made for a very different table setting.

Everyday crockery was obtained in the same way. The eclectic mix of peanut butter glasses and sparkling crystal was particularly appealing.

An electric kettle, toaster and two large pressure cookers, were wonderful presents, as was a supply of towels and bed linen. Mum also gave me three triangular saucepans, made to sit together in a circle, which were surplus to her requirements.

A wide range of gifts from the kitchen evening, plus a grocery shop that I had done, meant we were well set up in that department.

The wash house doubled as a tool shed, and contained the motor bike, two bicycles, a push mower, sundry garden tools and Ken's tool kit as well as my clothes basket.

Butter was shipped from New Zealand in wooden boxes containing fifty six pounds. New Zealand white pine, *kahikatea,* was the timber used, because there was no smell to contaminate the butter. Before the advent of the present cardboard carton, butter boxes were readily available, and had a multitude of uses.

Against the bedroom wall adjacent to the kitchen, Ken built us a wardrobe. Each end was a pile of five butter boxes, lying on their sides and facing inwards to form shelves. Two lengths of ¾ inch water pipe were attached to the top of the top boxes; one at the front to carry a curtain, and the other in the middle for supporting clothes hangers. I used second hand drapes to make the curtains, and attached the ends to cover the boxes with large drawing pins. Curtain rings slid on the front pipe.

Our fruit cases soon became a bank of shelves against the scullery wall; again with a curtain in front.

During the first week I made a table cloth from a length of small patterned green and white gingham, and cut some of the remainder into two inch strips. These strips became a frilled edging for the net curtains I hung either side of the kitchen window. There was enough gingham left to make cushions for our chairs.

All my early years we had only had a coal range for cooking, and since I knew that that was what I would be using, I practised a little before we married. I was surprised to find that I was having trouble getting the heat of the oven right.

If the oven was hot enough to cook a tray of scones, the back row of scones would be burnt.

Closer examination disclosed that the top back corner of the oven was burnt through and one could see the flames dancing past when the door was open!

By only using about three quarters of the oven that problem was solved.

Our milkman had his own dairy farm. After he and his family had completed the morning milking, he would load the cans of milk on the back of his wee motor truck, and commence his milk round. It was necessary to have ones' milk billy [with the correct amount of money] out at the gate in plenty of time. He had measuring ladles hooked over the edge of the can and ladled the milk into each billy. This was a seven day a week service. Cream was also available.

After about two years there was a problem with milk money thefts, so milk tokens were introduced. Thereafter, whenever the cost of milk changed, so did the tokens, either in colour or shape.

The butchery and bakery businesses were combined. The bakery was in Leeston, and fresh bread and meat were available from the Southbridge shop five days a week.

There was also a weekly meat delivery from a mobile butcher's van.

There were two general stores, and each of those provided a weekly grocery delivery. The deliveries were made by school pupils on their bicycles, after school hours. One would phone the order through earlier in the day.

We did not have refrigeration, but we had a large square tin meat safe hanging on the coolest section of outside wall. The two side walls had large ventilation panels of fine wire mesh. On a very hot day, a jug of milk was kept cool by standing it in a dish of water in the safe. There was a double piece of butter muslin over it and into the water all round; evaporation did the rest.

The previous tenants had left some rhubarb and silver beet plants in the garden, and Ken's mother had surplus vegetables that she generously shared.

Ken dug over a good sized area, and as soon as seasonal conditions permitted, we got our own vegetable garden under way.

Social Life

As soon as Ken returned to Southbridge to work, he joined the volunteer fire brigade. They practised every Wednesday evening and of course were 'on call' twenty-four-seven.

During the first year after we married, while we were having dinner, Ken heard the fire siren [at that time it was a high pitched continuous note] He rode his motor bike to the gate, opened the gate, rode through and went back to shut the gate. Then he realized that the 'siren' was directly overhead.

The wind was moaning through the power lines at the same pitch as the fire siren. That was his speediest return from a fire call-out.

On Saturday mornings he put on his Scout leaders' uniform and assisted Dougall with the local Scout troop.

I attended Church at least once a month. While nursing in Christchurch I became used to attending whichever Church fitted in with my time off, and without giving it much thought, considered continuing to be interdenominational. I realized immediately that that was not going to work in a country district, and I continued to worship with the Anglican congregation, as I had at Waipara.

The Women's Institute and the Garden Club each had a monthly meeting with interesting talks and demonstrations. Ken's Mum was an active member of both, and I joined too.

When a badminton club began in Southbridge, Ken and I both joined, and for two seasons we played for the local team against the surrounding districts.

I had always been an avid reader, and with books, sewing, knitting, establishing a garden and running my home, I found plenty to occupy my time during the nine hours Ken was working each day.

Ken and I both had slightly offbeat senses of humour, and if something amused us, we were likely to dissolve into a combined fit of giggling.

There was a shop in Christchurch that we used to frequent, until the day that the proprietor made a remark that set us off. We beat a hasty and extremely undignified retreat, through the door and down the footpath, hopefully out of earshot before we exploded.

Unfortunately we were unable to shop there again, because every time we passed the door, we looked at each other and burst out laughing again.

1952

Just before Christmas we had a visit from my previous employer. The permanent nurse was almost due for her annual holidays and they were hoping that I would consider two weeks of relief nursing.

We agreed to help out, and the extra bit of income was a help for us too.

My brother Harold had just completed his primary education and a decision had to be made for high school. To attend either Hawarden or Rangiora high schools would entail a lot of daily travel. The third option was to come to Southbridge and board with us. The high school was one mile's bike ride away.

At the beginning of February Harold came to live with us.

We had already obtained two more kitchen chairs, and my parents supplied a stretcher bed and a tallboy for Harold. With a ten years age gap, the relationship was somewhere between that of son and brother.

For Harold, the biggest difference would have been like that between youngest and oldest son. A transition he now had to make. He now says that he suddenly learned to eat what everyone else was having—or go hungry.

At lunch time he could bike home or take a cut lunch to school in the morning.

If Ken was working locally he always came home for lunch—sandwiches were not his favourite meal. Our main meal was always in the evening.

One lunch time Ken burst into the kitchen and gasped out "YOU SHOULD HAVE SEEN THAT"!

After he had crossed the road to our gate, he looked back at the traction engine that he could hear coming up the road. It was travelling along the grass beside the road, and Ken noticed that the driver had his head down, fully engrossed in making an adjustment to some of the controls. A few chains further along, a car was parked on the grass. The engine was heading straight towards it. There was nothing he could do to attract the driver's attention.

As Ken watched in horror, there was a very slight alteration in the path of the engine, and it passed the car with inches to spare.

The driver still had his head down and was quite oblivious to the fact that his was not the only vehicle on that stretch of grass.

Bread

BREAD WAS BAKED IN TINS that were slightly narrower at the base, so the loaf would slide out easily.

This gave the loaf a distinctive shape; and above the tin the bread would bulge over the rim all round, so the top was always rounded, darker and more crusty.

There were two sizes of bread tin—one being half the size of the other. Two equal sized balls of dough were placed in each tin, and the loaf would easily pull apart in the middle.

A large loaf was the big one undivided. A half loaf could either be half a large, or a complete small loaf. A quarter-loaf was half of the small one.

An important part of the table setting was the bread board and knife. There could also be a bread fork for politely passing a freshly cut slice, or sometimes the 'cutter' would lift the slice on the point of the knife and place it on the proffered plate. With a large family, the person cutting the bread could be kept very busy.

They would also become very proficient, and would produce neat slices of the required thickness, from a loaf on which the cut side was perpendicular and cut straight across. I am not describing the effect I achieved [which was always a bone of contention in our house].

For making toast in front of the fire, the bread was cut thick enough to hold its shape when speared on a four prong toasting fork.

[I had made our fork while still at Manahune]. I used two lengths of heavy gauge lacing wire folded in half, and I stapled these to the top of the chopping block. With a fire poker inserted into the loops, I twisted the four wires together to form a neat handle, with a ring at the top for hanging. In deference to the axe when next used, I removed the staples before using pliers to shape and position the four prongs.

Our electric toaster would toast one side of each of two pieces of bread.

There was a double sided element in the middle, protected by vertical wires spaced to support a slice of bread.

On each side was a drop down flap on which to place the bread. When these were closed the bread began to toast. It was imperative to stay with the toaster if one did not wish to be summoned by a cloud of smoke and that familiar smell. When one thought it should be about ready, one opened out the two side flaps and turned the bread over. Pop-up toasters were being talked about, but we didn't see one for quite a few more years.

Ken's mother decided to upgrade her three piece lounge suite, and offered us her old one. Now we could furnish our lounge, and have somewhere apart from the kitchen to entertain our occasional guests.

Every item of furniture we acquired [whether old or new] was new for us and we relished each one.

The total amount of joy, as we gradually furnished our home, far exceeded what there would have been if we had had everything there at the beginning.

I now started to make a new rag mat to use in front of the hearth in the sitting room. All the floors in the house were of polished wood, except for the scullery and bathroom, which had linoleum.

Next Generation

IN THE AUGUST OF 1952 Dougall and Zita had a baby boy. A few weeks later it was confirmed that I was pregnant too.

There was now a new focus on my sewing, as I made suitable garments for myself, and began sewing gowns and knitting a layette for our baby. I also bought the wool and began knitting a baby shawl.

The time had come to upgrade our transport, and a good starting point was for a garage to house a car.

Ken spoke to our landlord, and he agreed to our using the corner of the paddock adjacent to our house section. This had a gorse hedge on the road frontage; and a wire fence on that side of the section.

A 'very tatty' gorse hedge formed the frontage of the section. This led to a ten foot wooden gate at the other end. In the middle of this hedge was a little wooden gate, opening onto a path that led straight to the front door. Beside this gate was the mailbox.

After another word with the landlord we had permission to upgrade the whole frontage. Out came the gorse and it was quickly burnt. The little gate was moved to the side close to the garage, and the rest of the frontage was levelled.

Among the discarded timber from Dougall's joinery work-shop, were a lot of cedar slats 3/8 in. by 2 in. These were of assorted lengths, and made a very nice herring bone fence, when attached to a framework of square posts with top and bottom rails.

Cars were imported preassembled and arrived in large five-ply cases. When disassembled these cases could be purchased. Ken bought two of them, and built a twenty by ten ft. garage, that was six ft. high. It had a gable roof [covered with Malthoid], a side door opening into the section, and double doors opening out to the road. This garage also gave us storage space for the lawnmower and my bottled fruit.

The work was completed by us forming a new path from the gate straight up the section beside the house, with a diagonal branch to the front door. We edged this path with bricks, and returned the original garden path to lawn.

Ken dug an 8ft. strip against the front fence, and we harvested a crop of potatoes from it before I turned it into a flower garden.

At this time Ken's current job was the upgrading of a commercial Garage in Leeston. This job involved the pouring of a large area of concrete floor. He particularly remembers it, because it meant shovelling shingle from the riverbed onto a flat-bed truck, then shovelling it off again. The next lot of shovelling was into the concrete mixer. Wheelbarrows transported the concrete to the slab of floor being poured.

The proprietor of the business had an agency for Morris cars and this led to our becoming the owners of a Morris minor tourer. Ken and his father flew to Auckland and drove the little car home. The Triumph motorcycle was the down payment.

Now whenever we travelled I knitted as we went, and much of the shawl was knitted on the way to Waipara and back.

<h1 style="text-align:center">1953</h1>

For Christmas 1952 we went to Manahune, and stayed for the rest of Ken's two weeks holiday. The Waipara Memorial Hall was being built and Ken took a 'busman's holiday' dwanging the ceiling.

Towards the end of the second week there was a lot of rain, and as we were going home on the Sunday, we found that the Ashley River had broken its banks and the road was impassable. We returned to Manahune and the Memorial hall benefitted from another week's assistance.

At the beginning of 1953 I once again did two weeks relief nursing, although I was six months pregnant. I told my employer then that this would be the last time. As we were returning home some young larrikins forced our car off the road by playing 'chicken'. It was very scary!

We had acquired a second hand pram and bassinette. I made drapes for the bassinette from some net curtaining. It was white with fine green spots. There was a firm mattress at the bottom, and a thin chaff mattress on top of that, then an under blanket and sheet. I had finished my sewing and we had bought cloth naps and woollen and cotton vests.

In the middle of April I tidied the vegetable garden and sowed broad beans ready for the spring. Early on the 26th I started having contractions and that night went into the Ellesmere hospital. At 11.30am on the 27th our first son was born.

I always knew that I wanted to name our first daughter Lenore Catherine, after my nursing friend, so we decided that Ken would name our first son. Garry Trevor seemed just right for our beautiful little son. As I held him in my arms I dedicated him to the Lord. Soon after, Ken arrived at the hospital and was as delighted as I was.

At that time the nursing procedure was to keep the mother in bed for a fortnight. After two weeks in bed it took several days to just recover from being treated as an invalid.

The disadvantage for any first child is the fact that every stage of their development is experimental for the parents.

One becomes a parent with some preconceived ideas, plus what one has read, plus all sorts of differing advice from all sorts of different people. Luckily babies are amazingly resilient, and as long as there is a modicum of common sense, with a good helping of instinct and love, most of these little people thrive. The Plunket nurses were a godsend as they regularly weighed the baby and reassured the mother.

The first three months was a time of insufficient sleep and the resulting tiredness, but from then on routines were established and life settled back on an even keel. At three months Garry was christened at the Glenmark church where we had been married.

Ken's mother once again decided to do an upgrade. This time it was the washing machine, and I am sure it was because she saw a need in our laundry. The agitator washing machine with electric wringer made my work so much easier. The daily boil up of naps could be done while the rest of the wash was in the machine.

During this winter Ken made himself a motor mower. It had a cut of two ft. and was powered by a Villiers motor. It had a metal frame and 12in. wheels with wire spokes and pneumatic tyres. The spring growth could now be taken in his stride.

Soon it was necessary to invest in a drop-side cot that we placed against the wall at the foot of our bed.

Gowns were long since outgrown and overalls suitable for crawling were my next project.

1954

KEN'S NEXT PROJECT WAS A flat-bed cart [mainly for Garry, but it was a good utility unit for many other purposes].

It had pram wheels and the front axle swivelled. It could be steered or pulled along by a rope attached to each end of the front axle.

Our garden was flourishing and beside the washhouse was a lovely sky blue hydrangea. I told Mum about it and gave her a cutting. Two years later she showed me a very healthy plant covered with bright pink flowers. Her soil was much too alkaline to maintain the blue colour.

In July 1954 Albert Arnold [named after his two grandfathers] joined our family. Fortunately his arrival was a little quicker than that of his brother. He was another lovely baby and I was itching to get home with him. This was to be the last time I had to spend that ridiculous two weeks in bed after a birth. Garry thought he was great and wanted to play with him straight away.

I quickly came to the conclusion that after the first child it was then survival of the fittest, as I removed lumps of coal, potatoes and other suitable toys [provided by his brother] from the bassinette.

With my second baby I was now more relaxed and flexible with time tables and have always regretted that it couldn't have been the same for Garry.

Garry was very eager to assist with the baby, and I found his ability to fetch and carry a very real help.

When he was three months old, Arnold was christened [again at Glenmark] and Harold once more joined our family. This time he had his own car and went to work with Ken.

Harold left school at the start of the May holidays in 1954, and stayed at Manahune until his sixteenth birthday in October.

He then returned to Southbridge and commenced his apprenticeship with Dougall.

Dougall and Ken's father owned a block of land between High St and Broad St in Southbridge. He had built his home on the north corner of the Broad St frontage, and Dougall's first workshop was just behind this house.

Dougall's business had now outgrown this building. He took over the High St frontage and built a much larger workshop on the north side. Behind the workshop he erected a building eventually intended for a large garage. As an interim measure, he divided it into rooms and installed all the amenities necessary for a very comfortable little cottage. With Zita and their two sons he moved into the cottage until their permanent home was built on the other side of the section.

On one of our visits to Manahune, Dougall joined us and we had a family discussion about the upgrade of the kitchen.

When we gathered there for Christmas we came prepared for a long stay. Auntie Margaret and Uncle Harold were there as well, and they camped out in an igloo tent on the front lawn.

After we had attended the early service at the Glenmark Church there was plenty of time to put the finishing touches to a sumptuous Christmas dinner. We lingered over the meal and were still sitting at the table when the boys came up with a great idea for the afternoon's entertainment. "Let's start taking the kitchen apart ready for the rebuild!"

Dad looked horrified, though he should have been used to his family by then!

Dad and the female contingent endeavoured to clear the table and do the washing up.

The rest of the party were busily setting up a temporary kitchen on the front verandah, and emptying cupboards and pantry ready for action.

1955

Margaret and Stan with their three children were living in the second house on Manahune. In the midst of all the turmoil Margaret had something else on her mind. Elizabeth Dawn didn't want to miss out on any of the excitement, and she made her arrival at the Waikari hospital on Boxing Day 1954.

Between Christmas and New Year the area was completely cleared ready for a new concrete floor.

The tank stand was moved, to enable the former wash house and coal shed to be rotated ninety degrees and moved back against the underground tank.

The wash house now became the pump shed, and the coal shed stored firewood and garden tools. The scullery, pantry and Grandma's room were completely demolished. The coal range and its chimney were removed, and the old kitchen was sledged to a new position under the pine trees in the implement yard, where it became a very handy storage shed. Our makeshift kitchen was up and running, complete with electric stove and kitchen sink. There was cold running water to the sink, but the water drained into a bucket.

After the holiday period, Ken and Harold were joined by David Ford, and this trio did the carpentry work, with assistance as necessary provided by the Manahune men.

While the concrete floor was being poured, the weather was so hot that it was imperative to keep the new concrete covered with wet sacks to prevent it from cracking.

The hot weather also caused a desperate need for extra fluids for the work force. Mum had an active ginger beer bug and we set up a ginger beer factory. Every day I would make a new batch, and bottle it into old beer bottles.

We scrounged these bottles from anybody who had them, and finished up with four or five dozen. We had also acquired the gadget for putting on crown bottle tops.

During this time we had a visit from the vicar.

We entertained him to afternoon tea in the midst of all these bottles. We mused on what he might have been thinking as he went on his way—"tut-tut, if I hadn't seen it with my own eyes, I would never have believed it"!!

The new area was matched into the original house, and three feet from the original wide hallway, added extra length to the new kitchen living room. The toilet door was originally on the same wall as the bathroom.

The length of the toilet was now reduced to allow access to the new laundry. This laundry also contained a shower. Opposite the bathroom was the site of a new linen cupboard. Once the building was complete, a concrete courtyard was poured with a step up to the drive way. Concrete blocks formed a low wall round the courtyard.

When we returned to Southbridge, Ken was glad that he now had a motor mower to help return the wilderness to a lawn.

At Easter, Dougall and Ken took the Scout troop camping at Momorangi Bay, in the Marlborough Sounds. Garry, Arnold and I spent the time with Zita and her two boys.

They had not yet moved to their new cottage. Garry, as an intrepid explorer, did the rounds of the section and showed his older cousin all the escape exits under and through the boundary fence. Fortunately for Zita, they made their move to their securely fenced cottage soon after.

Harold joined the fire brigade and both he and Ken helped build the fire engine that was completed that year. The next project was the fire station. They laid the concrete blocks for one wall, and were going to pour a concrete pillar to complete the wall the following weekend.

During the week there was a north-west gale, and that wall blew over; so it was back to square one.

When Christmas came, we were back staying at Manahune again. Mum was revelling in her modernized and spacious home. It was so much more convenient, and I think she wondered how she had managed so long with the way it had been.

Dad loved it too. His original reticence was understandable, because it was hard for him to let go of his original home, and the memories of his mother and brother, that had been such an integral part of it.

For this Christmas Auntie Margaret had knitted a rotund orange dog for Garry.

Its name was Angus and I guess it did bear some resemblance to a Scottish terrier.

Garry sat under the table and unwrapped his gift. Then he played with the paper, completely ignoring Angus. Auntie Margaret looked very disappointed.

Along came Arnold, and it was love at first sight. From then on he and Angus were inseparable and Garry really enjoyed that wrapping paper.

Grandparents

EARLY IN 1955 KEN'S PARENTS had the front of their verandah enclosed with a glassed wall. This formed a nice conservatory for growing pot plants and relaxing in the sun.

A large craft room opened off the back wall of the conservatory.

At the end beside the toilet was a good sized storage area for garden tools and firewood, with an outside door opening onto concrete steps. At the other end, adjacent to the kitchen and laundry, there was another outside door, also with its steps.

The Dougall grandparents were reaching the stage where they couldn't live on their own, so they came to Southbridge and moved in with their eldest daughter and son-in-law [Ken's parents]. They made good use of the conservatory and enjoyed getting to know their great grandsons.

Grandma had several minor heart attacks during that year, and I assisted with her nursing care. Finally she became bedridden and passed away the following year.

Grandad lived for several more years.

Although he was having memory problems, he lived a reasonably active life. He enjoyed pruning the fruit trees and cutting all the prunings into suitable lengths for kindling wood.

He stacked these neatly against the wall in the woodshed and Ken's mum had many years supply of dry kindling. When he was not working with fire wood, he liked to sit in the sun on the steps outside the woodshed. He would have his walking stick beside him, and whenever one of the children walked past he used the hook end as a crook to catch round their legs. It was a game they enjoyed playing with great Grandad.

Grandad had a very thick head of hair right through his old age. One day hair was being discussed, and he mentioned what hairy legs he had. He reached down and pulled up his trouser leg to show us. His eyes opened wide with amazement as he looked at that bare leg and said "Well they were, the last time I looked at them!

New House

In 1956 Dougall was building his home beside his workshop. When it was nearly finished he asked us whether we had considered building our own home.

We hadn't—but after four years living in the old house, we had some very definite ideas about what we would like in our home.

We did not realize that with a State Advance loan at that time, it was possible to build a small house, and only pay back the loan at the same amount per month that we were already paying in rent. We had the advantage that the Love parents were giving each of their sons a free half acre section.

Dougall suggested that we sketch out the plan for the house we would eventually like to own.

The house we were in, would have been built about seventy years earlier. Borer beetles had taken it over as a very desirable residence, and their presence was obvious. Neat little holes adorned some of the exposed woodwork, and were even through the wallpaper in places. The floor was riddled with borer, and fresh activity was very evident as I swept up the little mounds of ground wood that appeared each day.

There was very good reason for not bringing any new furniture into that house.

One day we both sat down on the same side of our bed. We had that sinking feeling, as the leg of the bed immediately went right through the floor. From then on there was the side of a fruit box tacked over the hole, and our bed migrated over it, six inches nearer the window.

The scrim beneath the wallpaper was detaching itself from the underlying wood.

There were large balloons of wallpaper hanging six inches or more below the ceiling in all of the rooms. Whenever there was more than a gentle breeze blowing, the walls came alive, as the paper moved gently in and out in time with the gusts. The same gusts also intruded between some of the floor boards and around some windows and doors; making it rather difficult to keep our home warm in winter.

On the north side of the house there was one smallish window. Twenty feet away from the window, a macrocarpa hedge had grown to the height of fifteen feet. This effectively shut out the winter sun.

Other areas where I could see 'room for improvements'; were the little matters of the 'outside toilet' and the lack of inbuilt storage space. Hot water in the laundry and an electric stove also had their appeal.

We gave some thought to the initial plan, and decided to make the rooms a reasonable size, and allow for a complete room as a later addition. This gave the square footage that could be built for the loan we could afford. There was also a 'suspensory' loan of 400 pounds that would not have to be repaid so long as we lived in the house for four years.

Ken drew up the plan and Dougall added the specifications. We arranged with Ken's parents to have the section immediately behind their house, as we both liked the idea of a back section. When Ken submitted the plan to the Council, there was some demurring.

One of the councillors did not approve of back sections ['they led to slums'].

A slum was not what we had in mind, and we argued our case. Finally we had permission to proceed.

A fifteen foot driveway was cut through, beside the existing house section.

It was widened to form a good sized turning area where Dougall's first workshop had been. Then Ken boxed and poured a four foot wide concrete path to connect the drive to the new house. A cattle stop at the road end eliminated the need to open and close gates.

Our new entrance way was only a few chains away from where we were living—on the opposite side of the road—so it was easy for me to take the boys and, keep Ken 'company' while he worked, or assist where I was able. By this time there was another baby on the way.

For each of the houses they built, Dougall's workmen were very versatile. They profiled, boxed and poured the foundation [including carting the shingle and mixing the concrete]. Then they dealt with the piles, bearers and floor joists. The framing was made up on site. They pitched the roof and laid concrete blocks or Summerhill stone.

They dealt with the drain laying and did the plumbing. The only things they didn't do were the electrical work and the internal plastering, paper-hanging and painting.

Dougall made all his own joinery and the carpenters installed all the kitchens and other units.

Our home was of brown and cream Summerhill stone. The roof extended over a concrete terrace that was overlooked by a side window from the kitchen, and by glass doors and windows the full length of the lounge and sunroom. In the corner below the kitchen window [set into the terrace] was a free shaped sand pit. This proved to be a very real asset, and when it was finally out grown, I turned it into a sheltered sunny garden, that even grew a tamarillo.

All the north facing walls of the kitchen, plus the living and sun rooms were full of windows. The living room was twenty ft. by sixteen ft. The sun room was ten ft. by sixteen ft. They were separated by fold-ing rimu doors that could be opened right up to form one big room.

At this stage we had other plans for the sun room. Because we had left the building of one bedroom to a later date, Ken's intentions were to put in a temporary partition across the room and build in bunks on each side.

On the south wall of the living room there was a square window. Below that window was a ten foot mantel piece over a low wall of grey Summerhill stone. Set into one end was an open fire place with a wood cupboard adjacent. The wood cupboard had a small door on the outside wall for easy filling. Randomly, between the stones, were mirror lined recesses that could contain small ornaments.

Between the mantel and ceiling, over the wood cupboard was a storage cupboard, and beside the wood cupboard, a book case had been built in.

In the corner between the window and the kitchen door, a built in desk enabled supervision of the sandpit whilst answering the phone.

The kitchen had an island bench with a hanging cupboard above it. The bench continued with the sink under a window and the stove on the other side of the u shape. A short section of bench separated the stove from a built in safe. This large cupboard had removable slatted shelves and was ventilated to beneath the floor and above the ceiling.

Between the island and the sandpit wall was the area we had reserved for a large dining table. Built in window seats [with storage room under lift up lids] lined the two walls under the windows.

The internal laundry door opened out from the kitchen; and beside that door was the incinerator. That had a wet back to boost the electric water cylinder in the linen cupboard beside it.

The laundry contained a stainless steel tub and a drop down ironing table. There was an outside door opening into a porch that accommodated raincoats and gumboots, and had a ramp down to the path below. Another door opened into the toilet.

On the other side of the toilet a sliding door led to the bathroom. The hand basin had a cupboard beneath, with a drop down door that formed a step, for little people to reach the basin. There was a short bath tub and a shower cubicle. At the end of the bath nearest the door opening into the hall, the wall formed the back of a coat cupboard, also opening into the hall.

The master bedroom was next to the bathroom, and its door was opposite that of the kitchen. The other hall door opened onto concrete steps at the front of the house. The house wall beside the front door was covered with Durock sidings, because this was intended as a temporary wall that we would build on to.

1956

THE NEW HOME WE WERE building contained features that were several years ahead of their common usage. Some of our ideas appeared in most of the locally built houses thereafter.

We extended our passion for built in storage to the bedroom. As well as floor to ceiling cupboard and wardrobe, with dressing table and drawers incorporated, we also built in the bed. The head board was part of an eight inch deep cupboard, with a shelf on top and sliding doors in front. Under the sprung wire base was a sheet of hardboard to catch the bedding dust and fluff. It was reasonably easy to clean with the vacuum cleaner. There were sliding doors each side and at the foot of the bed base.

The back wall of the dressing table recess was lined with mirror.

The window wall faced east and caught the morning sun. The window area was about eight foot wide by five foot high.

Even the toilet was not immune to our inventions. By dropping the ceiling, space was available for a suit case cupboard above it. That was accessed from the laundry. We painted the toilet ceiling black, and the visual recession meant that very few people noticed the reduced height.

Continuous fibrous plaster lined all our walls. The sheets were six foot wide and the length of each wall. In the entrance hall there was an ornamental recess, which had been moulded into the plaster when it was manufactured. I usually kept a fresh arrangement of flowers sitting on the under lit, glass shelf in the recess.

Anyone who has already read this far, should not be surprised to hear that our home was mainly decorated in various shades and tones of green. We found a wall paper that we loved for the hall. It was off white, with a reasonably sparse pattern of ivy leaves apparently creeping all over it. For the recessed wall, the ivy pattern was backed by a non-obtrusive trellis pattern.

Surrounding the house we were renting, were paddocks that were used by our landlord mainly for cropping. Part of the time they lay fallow and I had no qualms about wandering over them. Because they were well away from overhead power lines, they were a good place to introduce Garry to the joys of kite flying.

He must have caught the kite flying bug, because a good few years later he and his brothers were still flying kites over this piece of land. The main difference was in the size of kite. Theirs was over six foot tall, and attached to hundreds of yards of binder twine.

There was talk of a necessary apology to a neighbour, for spooking his team of horses, by this giant kite swooping over them.

In the summer of 1956, a crop of potatoes was sown in the part of the paddock to our north. It grew well, and in the late winter it was mechanically harvested. Soon after that harvest there was a reasonable fall of rain.

A six months pregnant young woman looked over the fence and saw potatoes scattered all over the worked ground. "What a waste!" She rang the landlord and asked permission to pick up the potatoes. He was more than happy to have them cleared away before they started to grow.

With a bucket and some sugar bags, I started to pick up potatoes, and drag the partly filled bags to our boundary fence. Just inside the fence I had a pile of large sacks that I proceeded to fill. It took several days to pick them all up, because there were still all the routine chores to do, and the boys to look after.

A filled sack contained 125 pounds of potatoes, and I finished up with eight of them. We sent them to the produce market in

Christchurch, and they sent us a very nice cheque! With this wind fall, we were able to have a 'formica' topped dining table custom made for our new kitchen. The chromium plated legs were set back to allow easy access to the window seats on two adjacent sides of the table.

This dining area was completed with cushioning; that was my next project.

For the cushions, darkish red vinyl was obtained from an automotive upholsterer. I used strips of this, folded over a length of fine cord, to make piping for round the top and bottom edges. The sides were four inches high and one edge was closed with a zip. We found fairly firm, four inch deep sponge rubber. There was sufficient for the five cushions that padded the full length of the window seat. The cushions looked well, and were robust enough to outlast the boisterous years and games of a large family.

Arnold was a very busy and enterprising twenty seven months old. He managed to get hold of a box of matches, and before I discovered what he was up to, he had chewed the heads off several of them. I got someone to drive us to the local doctor's surgery.

It was necessary to wash out his stomach, and I held him on my lap and restrained him during this procedure. Afterwards his health appeared to be fine, and he soon got over the indignity of his treatment.

I was completely drained, and I sat on the edge of the terrace at our new house [where Ken was working] and just supervised the boys at play, until it was time to go home and get tea ready.

Next morning I woke up with the worst migraine I have ever had—before or since. I have no idea who looked after the boys and prepared meals for Ken and Harold that day—but it certainly wasn't me.

The following month there was more drama. Two little boys were supposed to be in their beds. Suddenly there was a bump and a loud cry from the bedroom. I opened the door and picked up a little boy with blood pouring from his lip.

He had fallen off Garry's bed [where he shouldn't have been] and had put a tooth right through his lip. Ken and I took him to see the after-hours duty doctor in Leeston. I held Arnold in my arms and the doctor leaned forward to look at the lip, while he soothingly said "What a dear little girl." That 'dear little girl' drew back his arm and punched the doctor on the end of his nose.

The doctor's forbearance was amazing, as he, rather warily, continued his examination and treatment of the lip.

Our Southbridge doctor was going to retire shortly after our new baby was born.

Mum had been a midwife, but her last case had been many years previously.

I asked Mum how she would feel about taking on another patient, if the doctor was happy about it, and was available for support.

Both Mum and the doctor were agreeable, and it was all on for a home birth.

About the middle of November the doctor delivered an autoclave drum of sterilized equipment to our house. We put two single beds in the sitting room [one each for Mum and me.] Mum came to stay on the 18th.

During that night I knew that things were under way.

Soon after 11am Mum rang the doctor, and when Ken and Harold came home for lunch at midday, they were able to greet our very new daughter.

As I settled down for a well-earned rest, I heard an excited voice at the telephone in the hall, telling the family

"It's a Lipstick Job!

Yes the boys have a little sister."

www.ingramcontent.com/pod-product-compliance
Lightning Source LLC
Chambersburg PA
CBHW071203300726
48975CB00004B/1273